EXTREME JOBS

Divers

Tony Hyland

Smart Apple Media

This edition first published in 2006 in the United States of America by Smart Apple Media.

Smart Apple Media
2140 Howard Drive West
North Mankato
Minnesota 56003

First published in 2005 by
MACMILLAN EDUCATION AUSTRALIA PTY LTD
627 Chapel Street, South Yarra, Australia 3141

Visit our website at www.macmillan.com.au

Associated companies and representatives throughout the world.

Library of Congress Cataloging-in-Publication Data

Hyland, Tony.
    Divers / by Tony Hyland.
    p. cm. – (Extreme jobs)
    Includes index.
    ISBN-13: 978-1-58340-744-8
    1. Deep diving–Juvenile literature. Divers–Juvenile literature. I. Title.

VM984.H94 2006
627'.72–dc22   2005056802

Edited by Ruth Jelley
Text and cover design by Peter Shaw
Page layout by SPG
Photo research by Legend Images
Illustrations by Melissa Webb

Printed in USA

Acknowledgments
The author is grateful for the assistance provided by Stephen Henderson, Craig Elstone, Paul Bowers and Mike Thomas in providing background information for this book.

The author and the publisher are grateful to the following for permission to reproduce copyright material:

Cover photograph: Underwater diving, courtesy of Peter & Margy Nicholas/Lochman Transparencies.

© Steven M. Barsky, p. 23 (both); Australian Picture Library/Corbis, p. 21, 25; Coo-ee Historical Picture Library, p. 12; Josephine Hyland, pp. 9, 19 (both), 27 (both); Getty Images, p. 28; Frederick Florin/AFP/Getty Images, p. 24; Getty Images/Time Life, p. 13 bottom; Eva Boogaard/Lochman Transparencies, pp. 4, 20, 30; Clay Bryce/Lochman Transparencies, p. 15; Jiri Lochman/Lochman Transparencies, pp. 16, 17; Peter & Margy Nicholas/Lochman Transparencies, pp. 1, 8, 13 top; Gerhard Saueracker/Lochman Transparencies, pp. 6, 10; Alex Steffe/Lochman Transparencies, p. 5; Photolibrary.com, pp. 14, 26; Photolibrary.com/SPL, pp. 7, 11, 22; Picture Media/REUTERS/ Jim Bourg, p. 29.

6/07

Contents

Glossary words
When a word is printed in **bold**, you can look up its meaning in the Glossary on page 31.

Do you want to be a diver?

Take a deep breath and step into a new world—the world beneath the sea. This is a world of wonder and adventure, and sometimes danger.

Many people will never go under the sea. Yet, every day some people climb into their diving gear and set off for a day's work. Some divers search for pearls. Others study fish or investigate shipwrecks. Even welders and carpenters work under the sea.

Diving is an extreme job. Divers can get cold and wet. The work is sometimes hard and can be dangerous, but it is also an adventure. Most divers love their work, and would never give it up.

Perhaps you could be a diver one day.

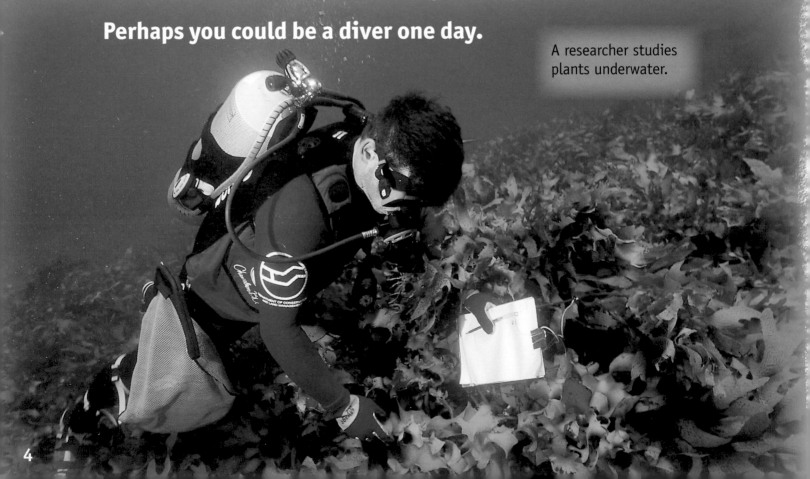

A researcher studies plants underwater.

Breathing underwater

Modern divers have two ways of breathing underwater. They can breathe air from air tanks strapped to their backs. They can also have air supplied through a long hose connected to a pump on the surface.

Divers who wear air tanks are called **scuba** divers. Scuba stands for Self-contained Underwater Breathing Apparatus. Some working divers wear scuba gear. People diving for fun wear scuba gear. Scuba divers can stay underwater for up to one hour.

Divers who have air supplied to them from the surface are called surface-supplied divers. The air is pumped from a boat or platform on the surface. Many working divers use this system. Surface-supplied divers can stay underwater for a long time.

Surface-supplied divers have air pumped into their diving helmets.

EXTREME INFO

Air supply

One air tank lasts about 30 minutes. Divers use more air in deep water, so some divers wear two tanks. When the air supply runs low, the diver goes back to the surface.

Diving gear

Scuba divers wear gear that lets them work underwater for up to an hour. They can dive to about 100 feet (30 m) underwater and wear lead weights to help them sink down.

flippers

air tank

snorkel

wetsuit

mask

gauge

regulator

Scuba divers wear gear that will help them to swim and breathe safely underwater.

- The air trapped inside the mask helps divers to see clearly underwater

- A **snorkel** allows divers to breathe near the surface of the water, without using air tanks

- Flippers, or fins, help divers to swim faster

- A wetsuit, made of a rubbery foam material called neoprene, helps divers to keep warm

- Steel or aluminum air tanks hold **compressed** air

- Divers breathe through a regulator, which controls how much air flows out of the tank. A **gauge** tells how much air is left in the tank

- A buoyancy compensation device (BCD) is an inflatable vest. Divers pump air into it to help them rise, or let air out to sink

Surface-supplied divers

Surface-supplied divers work for long periods, often in very deep water. Their equipment looks quite different than scuba gear. Surface-supplied divers wear a waterproof dry-suit and heavy rubber boots. If they are working in extremely deep water they wear an **atmospheric diving suit.**

- The diving helmet is sometimes called a hard hat. The air fills the helmet, so divers can breathe without a mouthpiece. The helmet includes a microphone, so that divers can speak to the crew on the surface

- The dry-suit or atmospheric suit prevents any water from getting in. Divers often wear warm clothes under these suits. In very cold water, divers wear a suit that has hot water pumped through it

- The air hose, communications line, and a strong rope join together to make the diver's **lifeline**

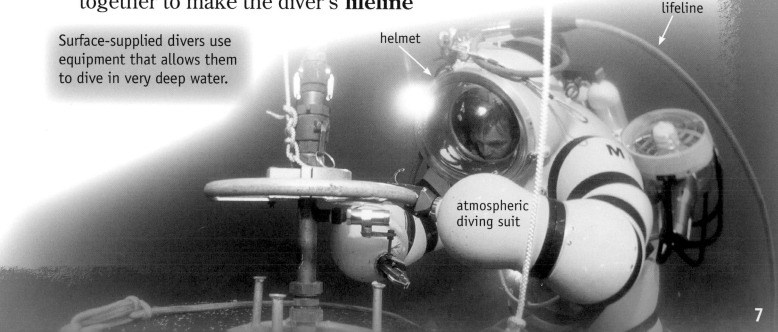

Surface-supplied divers use equipment that allows them to dive in very deep water.

helmet

lifeline

atmospheric diving suit

Risks and dangers

Working divers have to do their job every day. They cannot let the risks and dangers of diving stop them. Some of the risks for working divers are:

Pressure The pressure in deep water can cause pain and bleeding in hollow spaces in the body, such as the lungs, sinuses, and ears.

Cold Cold water drains away body heat. Divers wear special suits, hoods, and gloves to keep warm.

Air Normal air is good enough for most scuba diving, but can cause **decompression sickness** in deep water. Divers use a special mixture of gases, such as helium and oxygen.

Accidents If something goes wrong with machinery in deep water, divers can die before help arrives.

Bad weather A sudden fierce storm can interfere with the crew on the surface, rocking the boat and damaging equipment.

Shark attack Sharks have attacked divers, but this is not common.

Shark attacks are very rare.

Water pressure

As divers go underwater, pressure squeezes their bodies. The deeper they go, the stronger the pressure they feel.

Scuba divers do not normally go deeper than about 100 feet (30 m). The pressure at that depth is not a major problem. Surface-supplied divers can go much deeper, but they must rise to the surface slowly. Coming to the surface too quickly can give divers decompression sickness, or "the bends." Decompression sickness is a very painful illness and can be fatal. Divers suffering from decompression sickness are placed in a **recompression chamber.** Air is pumped into the chamber at high pressure, and then the pressure is very slowly reduced.

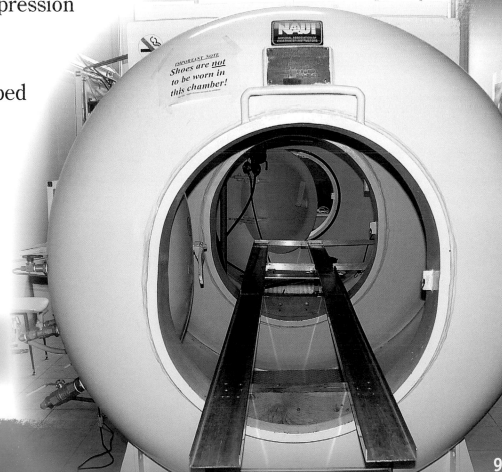

NAUI

IMPORTANT NOTE
Shoes are **not** to be worn in this chamber!

Recompression chambers are used to treat divers suffering from the bends.

Training

Most divers start their training by learning to scuba dive. Towns near the sea or large lakes often have a dive school, where people can learn to dive for fun.

Diving lessons start in a classroom, then the class moves on to practice in a pool. Here, the instructor can make sure that the students can dive safely. Finally, students go to the sea or a lake to practice **open water diving**.

Working scuba divers go on to more advanced courses. They learn how to dive in deeper water and how to take care of injured divers. They need to learn about water pressure and how to deal with it. As they pass each level, divers gain more advanced certificates.

Diving instructors teach the first lessons in a pool.

Advanced training

Hard hat divers do special advanced training courses to learn a whole new set of skills. They may need to dive in very deep water. This means that they must learn about new breathing equipment, including diving helmets. Divers learn how to adjust breathing gas for different depths. They also learn how to deal with water pressure.

Divers learn how to weld, cut metal, and use tools under water, such as **pneumatic drills**. All divers learn first aid. Some train to be diving medical technicians. They learn to deal with diving emergencies, such as decompression sickness. Working divers often travel out to oil rigs by helicopter. Knowing how to escape from a crashed helicopter is a very important skill that divers learn.

Advanced training is expensive, but divers with these skills are very highly paid.

Hard hat divers learn new skills, such as cutting and welding steel underwater.

Diving into history

For thousands of years, divers had no equipment. They could only stay underwater for a minute or two.

Some early divers used goggles made out of polished pieces of turtle shell. The first diving helmets were invented in the 1600s. The helmet sat on the diver's shoulders. If the diver bent over too quickly, the helmet could fill with water and the diver would drown.

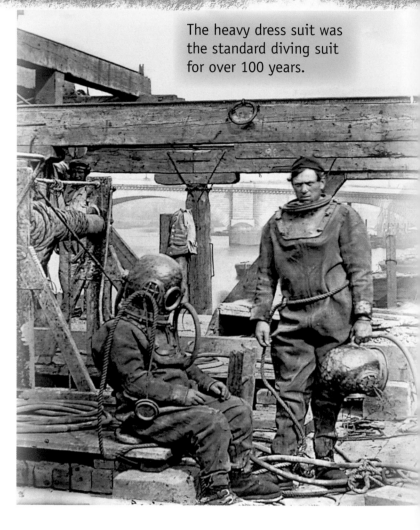

The heavy dress suit was the standard diving suit for over 100 years.

In the 1830s, Augustus Siebe invented the first modern diving suit. It had a large, round brass helmet, sealed to a canvas suit. Air was pumped into the whole outfit from a ship on the surface. Divers call this "heavy dress," because they wore heavy lead boots and heavy weights to keep them down.

For over a hundred years, all divers wore heavy dress suits. In some parts of the world there are still divers who use this equipment.

The invention of scuba

During World War II, a French diver, Jacques Cousteau, and an engineer, Emile Gagnan, invented the modern scuba system. At last divers could swim freely, without needing a lifeline. Navy scuba divers learned to swim silently up to enemy ships and sink them by attaching small bombs to them.

After World War II, many divers tried the new scuba gear and discovered that almost anybody could learn to dive. Diving became a popular sport. Today, thousands of people dive for fun and adventure.

Many people go scuba diving for fun.

EXTREME INFO

Jacques Cousteau

After World War II, Jacques Cousteau became famous for his new discoveries about the sea. He traveled the world in his ship *Calypso*, sending teams of divers to explore new places. He wrote books and made movies and television shows about diving.

Navy divers used the first scuba diving outfits.

Diving jobs

Pearl divers

Divers have collected pearls for thousands of years. Pearls grow inside oysters, which grow in warm, shallow ocean waters. Pearl shell is sometimes called "mother of pearl," and is used for jewelry and buttons.

Modern pearl divers work from large, well-equipped ships. The divers wear scuba gear, or use surface-supplied gear.

Pearl divers spend many hours in cold, murky water, diving up to 10 times per day. They collect oysters from the seabed in large mesh bags. On the ship, workers place a tiny bead of pearl shell into each oyster shell. Eventually, the oyster will form a pearl around this "seed."

Pearls form inside oyster shells.

Pearl diving history

One hundred years ago, pearl diving was a very dangerous job. Pearl divers in heavy dress worked in places such as the Caribbean, the South Pacific, and the Western Australian coast. Many pearl divers died in those days. Some drowned when their boats were caught in hurricanes. Others were attacked by sharks, or died when their equipment failed. Divers often had damaged lungs or eardrums, caused by diving too deep.

Today, pearl diving is a much safer job. Electronic devices such as timers and depth gauges help divers to judge their safe working depth. Divers understand their limits and take breaks to avoid permanent injury.

The old pearling boats were small wooden sailing boats, called luggers. Today's pearling ships are large, comfortable vessels, with modern safety equipment.

Pearl divers wear depth gauges on their wrist.

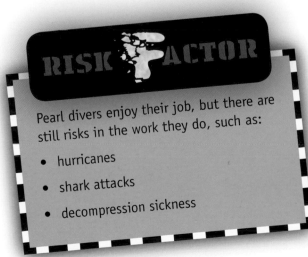

RISK FACTOR

Pearl divers enjoy their job, but there are still risks in the work they do, such as:

- hurricanes
- shark attacks
- decompression sickness

Diving jobs

Abalone divers

EXTREME INFO

Poachers

People who steal abalone are called poachers. They cause problems for abalone divers by taking too many abalone. Fishing inspectors try to stop poachers, but they are difficult to catch.

Professional divers collect large shellfish called abalone (ab-a-lo-nee) in shallow water. Most abalone is found in coastal waters. Diners pay very high prices to eat them in restaurants.

Abalone divers wear wetsuits and flippers. They breathe air pumped down through a hose from a fishing boat on the surface. The divers carry a wide, strong knife to pry the abalone off of the rocks. They load their abalone into mesh bags or plastic crates. They must work gently, as damaged abalone die quickly and can't be sold.

Abalone divers are well paid, but they can only work in good weather. Although their job is not difficult, abalone divers spend hours in the water every day, where it can get very cold.

Abalone divers collect abalone in large mesh bags.

Protecting abalone

In many parts of the world, abalone were almost wiped out by divers who took too many of them. In California, South Africa, and Argentina, divers took every abalone they could find. Today, abalone are protected. Ordinary divers are only allowed to take one or two abalone.

In Australia, divers pay millions of dollars for a license to collect abalone from one small area. They are not allowed to collect all of the abalone—they must leave enough behind to allow the abalone to breed.

Divers gather abalone by prying them off of rocks with a wide knife.

RISK FACTOR

Abalone divers earn a lot of money, but there are still risks in their work, such as:

- rough seas
- cold conditions
- shark attacks

Diving jobs

Diving instructors

Diving instructors are expert divers who have been diving for many years. They understand the dangers and the thrills of diving. Only qualified instructors can teach people to dive.

Diving instructors first teach their students in a classroom. Then they take the students to practice in a pool, and finally the students are taken to dive in a lake or the ocean. Diving instructors usually take small groups of students. They need to watch carefully, to ensure that each student is safe in the water. This is difficult when the class is 30 feet (10 m) under water.

Diving instructors also teach experienced working divers. There is always more to learn.

Diving instructors teach their students to communicate underwater using hand signals. They teach signals, such as stop, danger, and go down.

stop danger go down

Divers use these hand signals underwater.

PROFILE

Stephen Henderson

Diving instructor

Stephen Henderson runs
his own scuba diving school.

Job

I'm an open water scuba instructor on weekends. I
run my own dive shop during the week, where I sell
and repair diving equipment.

Experience

I've been diving since I was 19 years old. I
became a dive master, then qualified as a diving
instructor.

Most exciting experience

My most exciting experience happened when I was
working as dive master for a large group. I came
face-to-face with a dolphin 50 feet (15 m) under
water. It stood on its tail, watching me, and then
swam off. No one else saw it.

Scariest moment

I've never felt unsafe while diving, but a couple of
my students have. They thought they were running out
of air and panicked.
They grabbed my
mouthpiece, so I calmed
them down and got them
back to the surface.

Why I dive

Every time I dive I see
something different,
anything from a banjo
shark to a manta ray.

Stephen Henderson with a group of his diving students.

Diving jobs

A marine archeologist carefully explores a wreck, searching for clues about the past.

Marine archeologists

Marine archeologists are scientists who study the remains of sunken ships. They want to learn how sailors of the past lived and died.

Marine archeologists often dive to the wrecks of ships in the Mediterranean Sea. Ships have sailed these waters for thousands of years, and there are many ancient wrecks to be found.

Marine archeologists usually dive in scuba gear. They first mark the wreck into sections with string. Then they clear away mud from each section, uncovering items such as bottles, cups, or even parts of the anchor. As they find each item, they place it in a basket and send it up to the research ship on the surface. On the ship, researchers clean the items. They examine them closely, hoping to find out how people lived hundreds of years ago.

EXTREME INFO

Exploring in a mini-submarine

Archeologists sometimes explore wrecks in a mini-submarine. This allows them to stay underwater for several hours.

Exploring the *Titanic*

The *Titanic* was a large cruise ship that sank in 1912 in the Atlantic Ocean. In 1985, Robert Ballard and his team of marine archeologists discovered the *Titanic*. It was lying in pitch darkness, 12,500 feet (3,810 m) under the sea. The water pressure is too strong for divers at that depth. Ballard descended to the *Titanic* in the **submersible**, *Alvin*. His team did not disturb the wreck, but took many photos.

Since then, archeologists have explored the wreck of the *Titanic* many times. Now they travel in more advanced submersibles, with strong lights and mechanical arms. They must move gently, as parts of the wreck are rusting away.

As the researchers explore the ship they find hundreds of items, from tools to jewelry. Every item is cleaned up and put on display in museums.

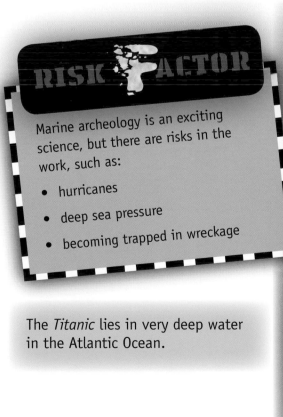

RISK FACTOR

Marine archeology is an exciting science, but there are risks in the work, such as:

- hurricanes
- deep sea pressure
- becoming trapped in wreckage

The *Titanic* lies in very deep water in the Atlantic Ocean.

Diving jobs

Marine biologists

EXTREME INFO

Chilly work

Some marine biologists study the sea life of Antarctica and the Arctic. They dive in special wetsuits because the water is so cold.

Marine biologists are scientists who study the plants and animals that live in the sea. Some study fish. Others are experts on whales, or on seaweed. They often work for a college or research center.

Many marine biologists train as scuba divers. Diving is a useful skill for marine biologists, because it lets them study marine plants and animals in their natural habitat. Marine biologists often work at sea on research ships. They collect specimens such as fish from coral reefs, or strange creatures from the deepest parts of the ocean. They examine the specimens under a microscope, and record their data on computer.

A marine biologist uses many tools. Underwater cameras, writing tablets, nets, and sample collection bottles are all useful equipment.

A marine biologist studies the plants in the ocean.

Kristine Barsky

Kristine Barsky is an experienced marine biologist.

Senior marine biologist

Job

I'm a marine biologist in California. I survey marine species underwater, including abalone. I give talks to school children, dive clubs, and scientists. I also help to write rules about fishing.

Training

I studied **zoology** and learned to scuba dive during my college years. Later I volunteered at a local **marine laboratory**.

Most exciting experience

While making a night dive at Catalina Island, I was joined by a harbor seal. It swam underneath me, almost touching, looking right into my face. It came and went throughout the dive.

Scariest moment

I thought I was alone and then suddenly a large shark was circling me. I was so surprised that I didn't panic, and it vanished as quickly as it appeared.

Why I dive

I love the ocean and everything in it. There are so many things to see and experience. I find it inspirational.

Kristine Barsky studies marine life with a video camera.

Diving jobs

Police divers

Police divers are full-time police officers who volunteer to become divers. They search underwater for clues to help police investigations.

Police divers cannot choose where they dive. Their job can take them to dams, caves, wells, and mineshafts, diving in freezing, dark water. Divers often crawl along muddy river beds, sifting mud with their bare fingers. Sometimes they find broken glass and other sharp objects!

Police divers use the latest scuba and surface-supplied diving equipment. Boats, wetsuits, and breathing equipment must be in top condition. Police divers can't take the risk that their equipment will fail.

Police divers often have to search for objects in drains.

Search and rescue

Police divers also work in rescue operations. They help when people are trapped by rising floodwaters. They can fly to the rescue by helicopter, or travel by rubber dinghy. When small boats are caught in storms, police divers are sometimes winched down from a helicopter to rescue the survivors. This is dangerous and difficult work. The helicopter pilot has to fly through wild, stormy weather. Then the crew must lower the diver on to the twisting, heaving deck of the boat. If they miss, the diver may end up in the sea, tossed around by huge waves.

Other rescue services also use divers sometimes. Navy and coastguard divers help in big rescue operations.

Coastguard divers help to rescue people by helicopter.

RISK FACTOR

Police divers work under difficult conditions, such as:

- diving in tight spaces
- diving in dark, murky water
- diving in rough seas and strong currents
- sifting through mud with bare hands

Diving jobs

EXTREME INFO

A dirty job!
Some onshore diving jobs are really unpleasant. One of the worst is repairing machinery in sewerage systems.

Onshore divers

Onshore divers work close to land, using surface-supplied gear. They work on underwater construction and maintenance. They even dive in dams and storage tanks.

Every day can bring different work for an onshore diver. They build and repair wharves and bridges. They do welding, concreting, and other underwater construction work. It's difficult to operate pneumatic drills and other tools underwater. Every movement is slower and more awkward than it would be on land.

On some jobs, divers work in muddy, cold water for hours. They wear warm clothes underneath a dry-suit to help them to stay warm. Surface-supplied divers never work alone. The surface crew keep the air supply going, and talk to the diver via the communication cable. One diver in full gear always stays on top, prepared to dive during an emergency.

Onshore divers do welding and other repair work close to the water's edge.

26

Craig Elstone is an onshore diver.

Craig Elstone

Onshore diver

Job

I run a marine services company. We repair wharves and jetties, and salvage sunken boats.

Experience

I've been scuba diving since I was 11 years old. I started working as a commercial diver when I was 21 years old.

Scariest moment

I was working at the bottom of a deep pit, about 30 feet (10 m) under water, when the pit collapsed. My air hose wasn't blocked, so I could breathe but I couldn't move. I just had to wait while my crew pumped away the mud and got me out.

Things I don't like about diving

There isn't anything I don't like about diving. There are dirty jobs, such as diving in sewage or cement slurry, which is a thin liquid cement. The job has to be done, so I just grit my teeth and get on with it.

Why I dive

I love diving. Every job is different. I travel to many places, wherever the work needs to be done.

Craig prepares to examine a jetty which needs repairs.

Diving jobs

Offshore divers

Offshore divers work in deep, cold ocean water, normally using surface-supplied gear. Sometimes they wear heated suits.

Many offshore divers work on oil rigs. Oil rigs are huge platforms in the ocean, where drilling teams pump oil from deep under the seabed. Divers check the underwater drilling machinery to make sure it is in good condition. They check for cracks in the oil rig's supports and repair them with underwater welding equipment. Oil rig divers usually travel out to the rig by helicopter. They work on the rig for a week, and then take a week off.

The work is hard and cold and it can be dangerous. Some oil rigs have burst into flames. Others have been flipped over in fierce storms.

Offshore divers inspect the support structure of oil rigs in deep water.

EXTREME INFO

Diving in a bell

Deep sea divers sometimes travel down inside a bell-shaped device, called a diving bell. This is open at the bottom, so the divers can just drop down into the water to work, and come back inside for a short rest.

Salvage divers

Salvage divers are also offshore divers. When a ship sinks, salvage divers are called in to help. People may be trapped, still alive, in air pockets inside the hull. Salvage divers can try to rescue them. Salvage crews have to move quickly.

Sometimes salvage divers work to raise a sunken ship to the surface. They repair some of the damage, and then pump air into the hull to raise the ship. They use welding torches and other equipment to cut their way through the sides of sunken ships. If the ship is too deep, they may send down small remote-controlled robots, called remotely operated vehicles (ROVs), which can go much deeper than humans. ROVs have lights and video cameras so that operators on the ship can guide them.

Crew members stop the diver's lifelines from getting tangled as the diver enters the water.

RISK FACTOR

Offshore divers often work in difficult and dangerous conditions. They must deal with:

- fire
- storms
- decompression sickness

Could you be a diver?

You could be a diver if you:

- have normal health, with no heart or lung problems
- are reasonably fit
- can swim 650 feet (200 m)—that's four lengths of a swimming pool
- enjoy being active outdoors
- are not afraid of water
- are not afraid of tight spaces.

If you learn a trade, such as welding or carpentry, you could learn to be an underwater construction worker. If you prefer to be a scientist, you could study marine biology or archeology. You'll spend a lot of time in the water.

Try snorkelling—you'll have fun, and it's a good way to see if diving will suit you.

Snorkelling is a good way to learn about diving.

Glossary

atmospheric diving suit	a hard-shelled diving suit used for very deep diving up to 2,000 feet (600 m)
compressed	forced into a small space
decompression sickness	a painful, sometimes fatal illness caused by nitrogen bubbles in the blood or joints
gauge	an instrument which measures something, such as the amount of air in a tank, or the depth of the water
lifeline	a deep sea diver's safety line, with air hose and communication cable
marine laboratory	a research centre where scientists can study ocean life
open water diving	diving in the sea or a lake, rather than a pool
pneumatic drills	drills that are operated by air compressor
poachers	people who steal protected animals
recompression chamber	a large, sealed tank used to keep divers under high pressure; used to treat divers suffering decompression sickness
scuba	a method of diving that allows divers to swim freely under water, while breathing air from an air tank
snorkel	a curved tube used by divers for breathing fresh air while close to the surface
submersible	a small submarine with thick glass windows
zoology	the branch of science for the study of animal life

Index